VALLEY FORGE MIDDLE SCHOOL
105 W. Walker Road
Wayne, PA 19087

ADAPTATION FOR SURVIVAL

MOUTHS

WRITTEN BY STEPHEN SAVAGE

Thomson Learning
New York

ADAPTATION FOR SURVIVAL

Books in the series

- EARS • EYES • HANDS AND FEET
- MOUTHS • NOSES • SKIN

Front cover: Young swallows in a nest, a child's mouth, and a crocodile in shallow water.

Back cover: A child's mouth.

Title page: Resting walruses displaying their canine teeth, or tusks.

First published in the United States in 1995 by
Thomson Learning
New York, NY

Published simultaneously in Great Britain by Wayland (Publishers) Limited

U.S. version copyright © 1995 Thomson Learning

U.K. version copyright © 1995 Wayland (Publishers) Limited

Library of Congress Cataloging-in-Publication
Savage, Stephen, 1965–
   Mouths / written by Stephen Savage.
         p.   cm.—(Adaptation for survival)
   Includes bibliographical references (p.   ) and index.
   ISBN 1-56847-351-6
   1. Mouth—Juvenile literature. 2. Animals—Food—Juvenile
literature. [1. Mouth. 2. Animals—Food habits.] I. Title.
II. Series: Savage, Stephen, 1965– Adaptation for survival.
QL857.S28   1995
591.4'3—dc20   95-7611

Printed in Italy

Picture acknowledgments

The publishers would like to thank the following for allowing their photographs to be reproduced in this book: Bruce Coleman Ltd.: *title page* (Johnny Johnson), 5 (above/Alain Compost), 6 (Gordon Langsbury), 7 (above/Paul R Wilkinson), 7 (below/Len Rue Jr.), 8 (below/Jane Burton), 9 (above/Erwin & Penny Bauer), 9 (below/Christian Zuber), 10 (above/Stephen J Krasemann), 11 (above/Jane Burton), 12 (above/M P L Fogden), 13 (Jane Burton), 14 (Michael Freeman), 15 (below/Charles & Sandra Hood), 16 (below/Kim Taylor), 17 (Jane Burton), 18 (Frank Greenaway), 19 (below/Kim Taylor), 20 (above/M. P. L. Fogden), 21 (below and above/Alan Stillwell), 22 (Jeff Foott Productions), 23 (above/Erik Bjurstrom), 24 (Hans Reinhard), 25 (below/Kim Taylor), 26 (left/Andy Purcell), 26 (right/Kim Taylor), 28 (Jeff Foott Productions), 29 (above/Kim Taylor), 29 (below/Dr. Frieder Sauer). Francesca Motisi: 25 (above). Natural History Photographic Agency (NHPA): 8 (above/G. I. Bernard), 10 (below/Pierre Petit), 11 (below/Martin Harvey), 12 (below/G. I. Bernard), 16 (above/Anthony Bannister), 19 (above/Anthony Bannister), 20 (below/Jany Sauvanet). Oxford Scientific Films (OSF): cover (top/Roland Mayr); 15 (above/Max Gibbs), 23 (below/Norbert Wu), 27 (Leonard L. T. Rhodes). Reflections Photo Library: 5 (below/Jennie Woodcock). Tony Stone Worldwide: *cover* (bottom). Wayland: *cover* (middle), 1.

Contents

Human Mouth	*4*
Carnivores	*6*
Herbivores	*8*
Beaks	*10*
Jaws	*12*
Fishy Mouths	*14*
Tube Mouths	*16*
Sticky Tongues	*18*
Fangs	*20*
Huge Mouths	*22*
Keeping Cool and Warm	*24*
Mouth Changes	*26*
Simple Mouths	*28*
Glossary and Further Reading	*30*
Further Notes	*31*
Index	*32*

Human Mouth

The tongue is useful for reaching food we might otherwise miss!

This is a diagram of the human mouth. More details are given on page 31.

The human mouth has many uses. We use our mouths for eating and drinking. At the front we have teeth for biting and tearing food. At the back, we have teeth for chewing. Although we breathe through the nose, we can breathe through the mouth if we are short of breath, using lots of energy, or if we have a cold.

The tongue also has many uses. As well as using it for licking food, we also use it when we chew our food. It has taste buds that tell us if the food we are eating is sweet, sour, salty, or bitter. We also use our tongues when we are speaking. As we open and close our mouths, the shape of the mouth and the position of the tongue help to form words.

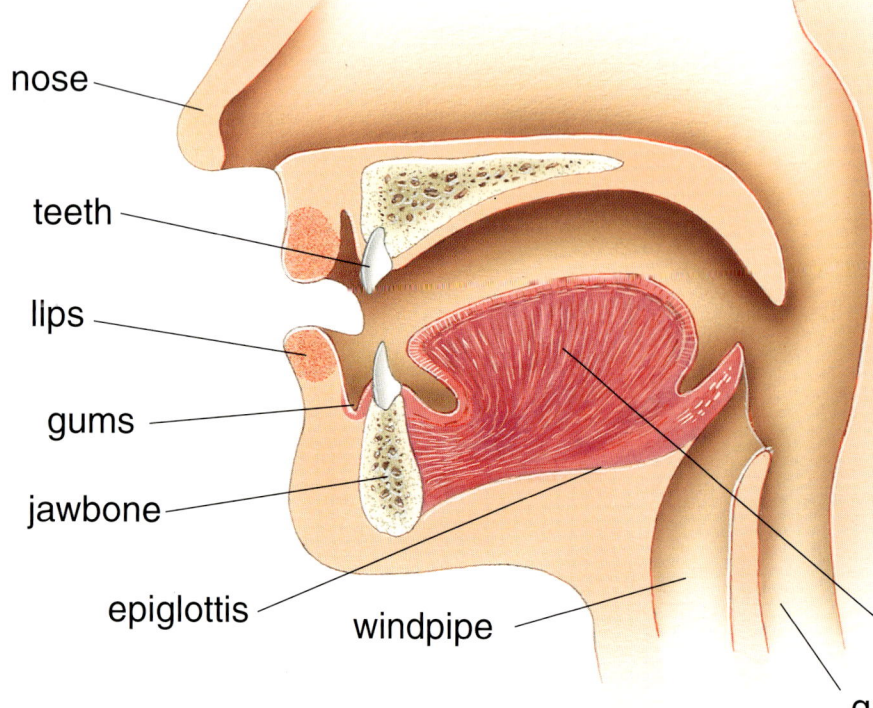

4

Humans are not the only animals to have mouths adapted to many uses. Many other animals have teeth and a tongue with taste buds and use their mouths for making sounds, cleaning themselves, and fighting, as well as for eating. As you will see in this book, however, the mouths of many animals are suitable for eating only one type of food, and some mouths are very simple indeed.

We use our mouths and lips to show other people how we feel. When we are happy we smile.

We also use our lips to kiss, as a greeting or sign of affection to members of our family or very close friends.

5

Carnivores

Carnivores, such as lions, tigers, wolves, foxes, and baboons, have mouths adapted to catching and eating other animals. Their strong jawbones and fang-like canine teeth are used to grasp and kill their prey. Like humans, they also have taste buds on their tongues.

Carnivores, like this tiger, use facial expressions and growling as a threat to others. The tiger's snarl reveals large, threatening canine teeth.

Just like the domestic cat, these lions are using their tongues to lap up water.

Some carnivores live in the sea. Killer whales catch fish and other sea mammals by hunting as a pack. They have been known to attack and eat seals, dolphins, and even large whales. The leopard seal regularly attacks and eats other seals and penguins. The sperm whale has teeth only in its lower jaw that it uses to catch and eat giant squid.

Some carnivores use their mouths to help them make sounds. This coyote is howling to keep in contact with others in the pack.

7

Herbivores

The mouth of a herbivore is adapted to eating grasses, plants, and fruit. Many herbivores have long front teeth called incisors with which to nibble grass and leaves from plants. They also have large back teeth called molars with which to grind their food before swallowing it.

Many large herbivores, such as the zebra and antelope, live together in herds as a protection against carnivores such as the lion and cheetah. These herds are always on the move. As the animals eat the grass in one area, they need to travel to find fresh grass elsewhere.

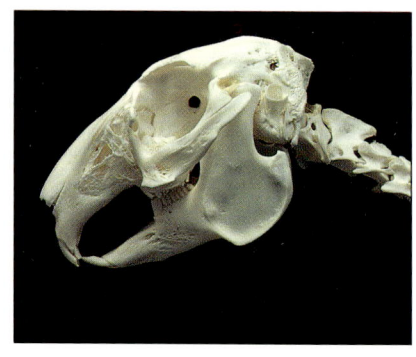

A rabbit skull, showing the incisor teeth at the front of the mouth and the molars at the back. Humans have similar teeth, but they are grouped together.

A herd of zebra roams the plains feeding on grasses. Like most mammals, zebras also use their mouths to help make sounds.

▲ *The black rhinoceros uses its upper lip to grasp the small branches of bushes that it bites off to chew slowly at leisure.*

▼ *The marine iguana dives underwater to feed on algae and seaweeds on the coast of the rocky Galapagos Islands.*

Herbivores come in all shapes and sizes and live in all kinds of habitats. Rabbits live underground and come to the surface to feed on grasses and plants. Monkeys live in trees and eat leaves and fruit. Some sea snails have sandpaper-like tongues with which to scrape algae from rocks.

Beaks

Birds of prey, like this peregrine falcon, use their hooked beaks to tear bite-sized pieces from the animals and birds they have caught. Humans use cutlery to help them eat food.

A bird's beak is its mouth. There are many different types of birds, and the shape of the beak depends on the type of food they eat. The blue titwillow has a short, pointed beak suitable for catching and eating insects and pecking at fruit. Eagles and owls have strong, sharp, curved beaks necessary for catching and eating small mammals or birds.

Birds that feed on sandy beaches, mudflats at the mouths of rivers, and shallow lakes have long beaks for catching creatures beneath the sand and under the water.

This godwit uses its long, pointed beak to catch marine worms and other small sea creatures living underneath the sand.

The macaw uses its strong beak to crack open nuts and seeds and as an extra limb to help it climb. It can also use its beak to preen itself or its mate.

Hummingbirds have long beaks with which to sip the nectar from flowers. Ducks have wide, flat beaks for sieving water and mud for food. Birds also use their beaks to help make their nests and to sing.

It is not just birds that have beaks, however. The duck-billed platypus is considered a mammal (even though it lays eggs), but it has a flat, leathery beak, shaped like that of a duck. The beak is sensitive to touch and is used to catch crayfish, worms, and frogs. Octopuses and squid also have beaks in the center of their tentacles that are used to break the shells of crabs and lobsters.

A pelican uses the pocket of stretchy skin beneath its beak as a fishing net.

Jaws

There are many different kinds of jaws. Our jaws (and those of other animals and fish with teeth) are the pieces of bone that hold our teeth. They are hinged so that they can open and close.

Many insects also have hinged mouth parts. These insect jaws are used for catching and holding food but also for a range of different tasks.

Snakes have jaws that they can unhinge to allow really large prey to pass down into their stomachs.

The leaf-cutter ants of South America use their jaws to cut bits of leaf and to carry them back to the nest to make compost. Fungus, which the ants eat, grows on the compost.

12

These stag beetles are using their jaws for fighting.

Some species of wasp use their jaws to chew up wood to make "paper" nests. Black worker ants have many uses for their jaws. They use them for feeding, for building and repairing the ant nest, and for carrying their eggs and larvae. South American army ants do not make a nest, but keep on the move guarded by soldier ants who use their large jaws in fights with other ants.

Dragonfly larvae have hidden jaws that they use for catching other pond creatures. Crabs and lobsters use their jaws for tearing their meals into small pieces.

Fishy Mouths

Like birds, fish have mouths adapted to the type of food they eat. Most sharks have sharp teeth for biting into large sea creatures. The grouper just opens its large mouth and gulps the fish down whole.

Goldfish and many catfish use their mouths like vacuum cleaners to suck up food from the bottom of ponds and rivers. An adult archerfish does the opposite: it can spit out a jet of water up to five feet to knock its insect prey into the water. Catfish have whiskers around their mouths to help them find food in murky water.

The forceps fish has a long snout to reach deep into rocky crevices.

The red-bellied piranha has sharp triangular teeth for eating flesh. Although each fish is quite small, a school of piranhas can strip the flesh from a large animal in a very short time.

Some kinds of fish use their mouths to make a nest. Three-spined sticklebacks collect pieces of underwater plant in their mouths to make their nest. Siamese fighting fish blow bubbles to make floating bubble nests for their eggs.

The mother mouthbreeder fish keeps her newly laid eggs in her mouth until they hatch. Once hatched, the tiny fish stay near the parent and dart back into the mouth at the first sign of danger.

Parrot fish have strong teeth that they use to bite off lumps of coral.

15

Tube Mouths

Some animals have tube-shaped mouths with which to suck up small creatures or liquids. Mollusks with two shells, such as clams and mussels, live on the bottom of seas and rivers. Instead of hunting for food, they continually suck water into their shells to feed on tiny animals and plants called plankton.

Butterflies and moths have tube mouths for sucking nectar from flowers (similar to a human using a drinking straw). The house fly has a short tube mouth. This fly pumps digestive juices from its mouth to liquefy parts of its food, which it then sucks up. Fleas have special mouth parts for piercing the skin and sucking blood from mammals and birds.

This white mussel has two feeding tubes. Water is sucked in through one tube, and tiny creatures are filtered out by the real mouth. The water is then forced out through the other tube. These feeding tubes are also used for breathing.

This butterfly's long tube-shaped mouth is good for reaching nectar. When not being used for feeding, the tubed mouth is coiled under the head out of the way.

Sea horses and other pipefish have long tube-shaped mouths. They hide in seaweed waiting for a shrimp or fish to swim by and then quickly open their mouths and suck up their prey.

Sticky Tongues

A common toad using its long, sticky tongue to catch a caterpillar. Its wide mouth allows it to swallow prey whole.

A sticky tongue is useful if your meal is small or moves quickly. A frog's sticky tongue is attached to the front of its mouth. The tongue is quickly flicked out to catch insects, worms, and slugs. The chameleon hunts its prey above the ground in trees and other plants. It shoots out its tongue to catch locusts and other prey.

Some mammals also feed using long sticky tongues. The aardvark digs its way into a termite nest and catches termites on its tongue, which is kept sticky with saliva. Although the human tongue uses saliva to keep it moist, is not sticky.

Woodpeckers also have long sticky tongues that they use to catch insects. Green woodpeckers often feed on ants by pecking a hole in their nests. A woodpecker's tongue also has a barbed tip like an arrowhead or the end of a fish hook that is used to spear insect larvae that bore into trees.

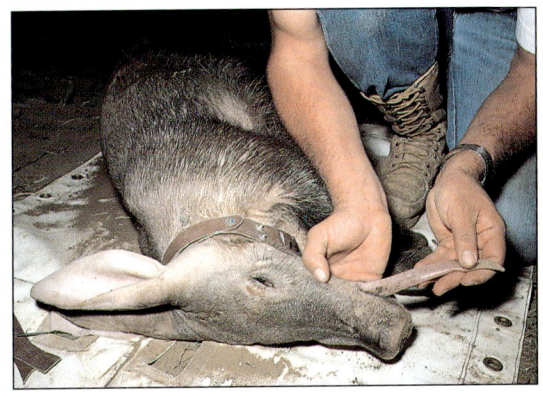

A scientist looks at the very long sticky tongue of an aardvark. The aardvark was put to sleep for a short time.

This green woodpecker is using its barbed and sticky tongue to hook out a grub from a small hole in a piece of wood.

Fangs

Carnivores that eat animals larger than themselves need to be able to overcome their prey without coming to harm. Some snakes have hollow fangs through which they inject poison as they bite their prey. The snake then retreats to a safe distance while the poison does its work. These snakes can also use their poison as a defense against attack from other animals.

This toad-eating snake is displaying its fangs as a warning.

Vampire bats have fang-like teeth that they use to scrape a wound in the skin of mammals such as cattle or horses. The bat then uses its tongue to lap up and suck up blood. Although vampire bats never drink enough blood to seriously harm an animal, their bite can transmit a dangerous disease called rabies.

The mouth parts of a tarantula, showing its black fangs

Spiders also have poisonous fangs for catching prey. The bird-eating spider includes small birds in its diet, while the water spider catches worms and small fish. The black widow spider of North America produces poison from its fangs that is 15 times stronger than that of a rattlesnake.

21

Huge Mouths

Large mouths are very useful for feeding on small creatures that are scattered over a wide distance. Whales, sharks, and some fish feed on small aquatic creatures, and a large mouth helps to catch food. Many large whales have no teeth but have hard bristles called baleen. These whales swim through the sea with their mouths open, straining the water for food as they close their mouths in the same way as humans catch fish by dragging nets through the water.

This group of humpbacked whales has worked together to form a circle of bubbles to trap its prey. As the whales close their mouths, seawater is forced through the baleen, but any small creatures are trapped and swallowed.

The large fins on either side of the devilfish's mouth are thought to channel plankton and small fish into its mouth.

The whale shark grows to 60 feet long and is the largest fish in the sea. Despite its huge mouth, the whale shark feeds on plankton and small fish. Some smaller creatures have a large mouth compared to their body size. The freshwater paddlefish from the Mississippi River system has a large mouth for feeding on plankton.

In the dark depths of the ocean, the deep-sea swallower catches fish with a huge mouth that takes up most of its head.

Keeping Cool and Warm

Many animals have body coverings—such as fat, feathers, or fur—that are adapted to keep them warm. In hot weather, or when they have made themselves hot by running, they have to find a way of cooling down. The mouth plays a vital part. Some mammals lick their bodies when they are hot. As the wetness dries it cools the skin. Some, such as cheetahs, dogs, and even humans, pant. Breathing out hot air from the lungs helps to cool down the body.

A crocodile's body temperature depends on the temperature of its surroundings. Crocodiles bask in the sun with their mouths open, not to lose heat, but to gain heat. The sun heats up the blood vessels inside the mouth, and the warm blood is circulated around the crocodile's body, enabling it to move more quickly.

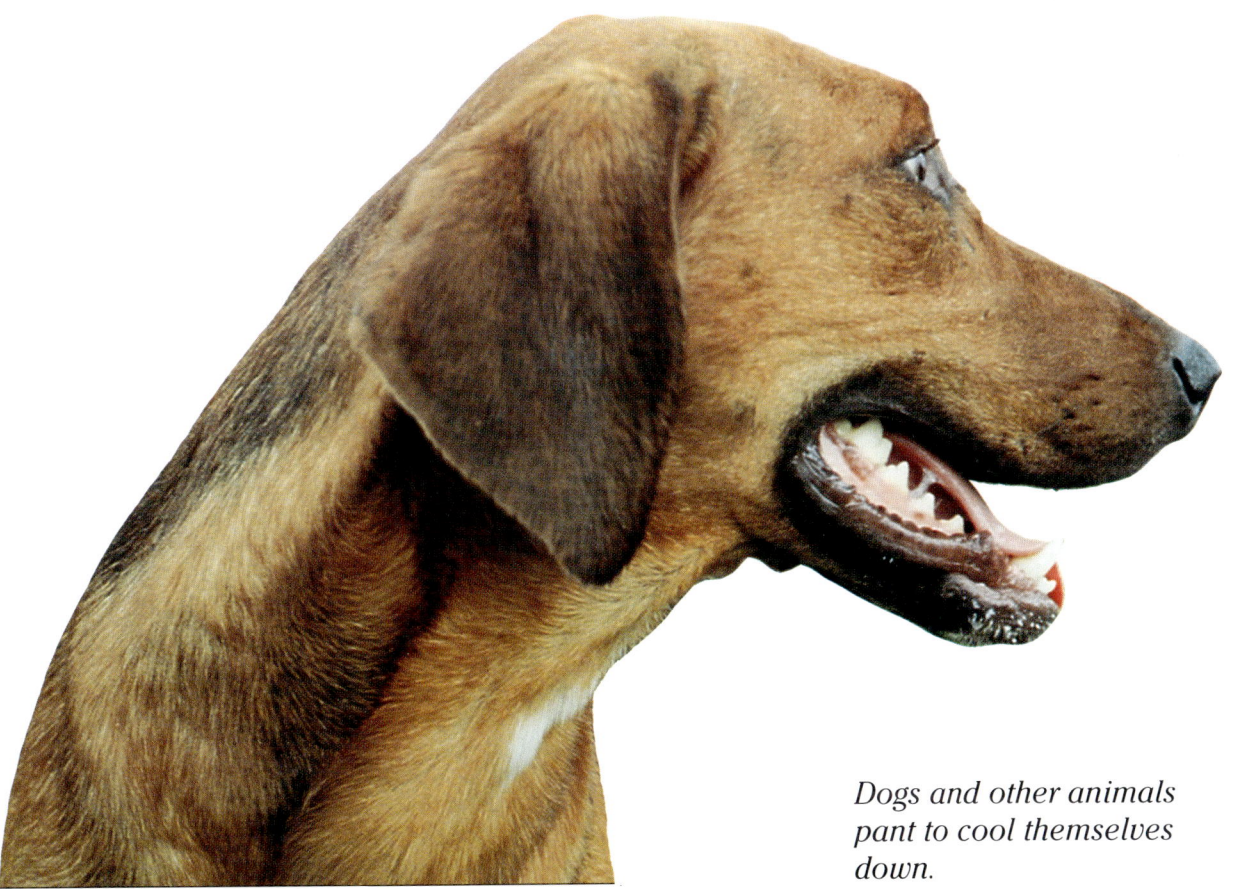

Dogs and other animals pant to cool themselves down.

Birds, which do not have sweat glands, can only lose excess body heat by sitting with their beaks open.

25

Mouth Changes

Some animals change shape during their lives and their mouths change as well. The caterpillar (a butterfly larva) has jaws for eating plants. When it becomes an adult butterfly, the jaws change into a tube mouth for sucking up liquids.

The mouth of a tadpole changes from a mouth for feeding on algae to a frog's mouth, with a sticky tongue.

Many mammals, including humans, are born without teeth. In early life, the young mammal feeds on milk provided by the mother. Human babies progress to special baby food before they are old enough to eat solid food. By then, they will have their first teeth. Walruses have enlarged canine teeth called tusks that become visible when a walrus is about a year old, and they continue to grow. The walrus that has the largest tusks is considered the boss.

Humans grow two sets of teeth, but some animals have more. Sharks have many rows of teeth, and when a tooth is lost, it is replaced by the one behind. A rabbit's front teeth grow in length throughout its life and are kept at their normal length by frequent chewing.

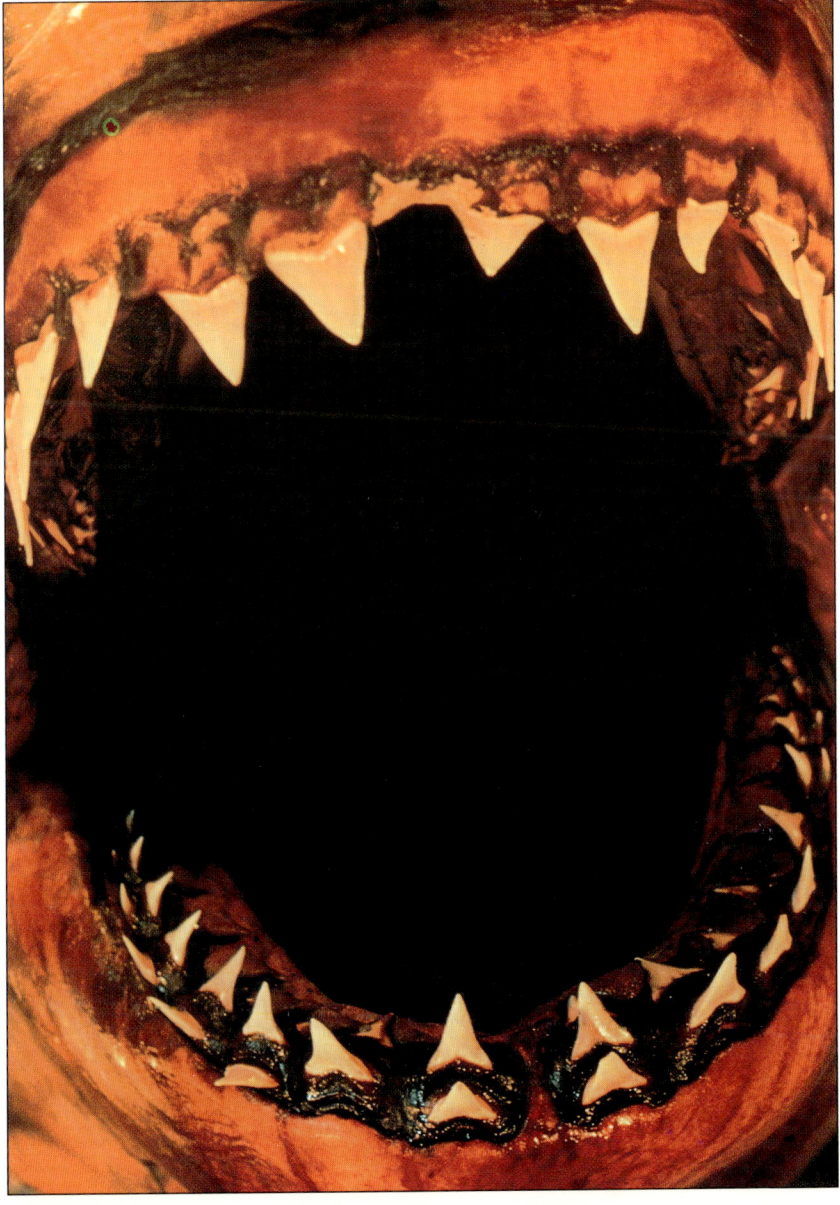

This close up of the teeth of a great white shark shows gaps in the row of outer teeth being filled by teeth from the second row.

Simple Mouths

Some animals have simple mouths that are really just holes in their bodies. The sea anemone passes food into its mouth and then ejects indigestible items out of the same mouth hole. A starfish is able to eat large prey such as shellfish by pushing its stomach out through its mouth and digesting its meal outside its body.

This sea anemone's mouth is in the center of the tentacles that are used for catching small fish and other sea creatures.

Earthworms travel through the soil by eating their way through it. They also feed on leaves that they pull underground. The marine lugworm lives beneath the sand and feeds on anything that falls into its U-shaped burrow. It digests anything edible. The rest passes through its body and is ejected onto the sand, making a worm cast.

The amoeba turns a part of its body into a mouth when it needs to, wrapping itself around its microscopic prey. Other microscopic animals have hairs that move in such a way as to create currents that direct food into their simple mouths. The simple mouths of these animals are adapted to their simple needs.

▲ Gardeners like earthworms because the worms eats their way through soil, breaking up the ground and allowing air to reach the roots of plants. Earthworms also produce their own natural fertilizer.

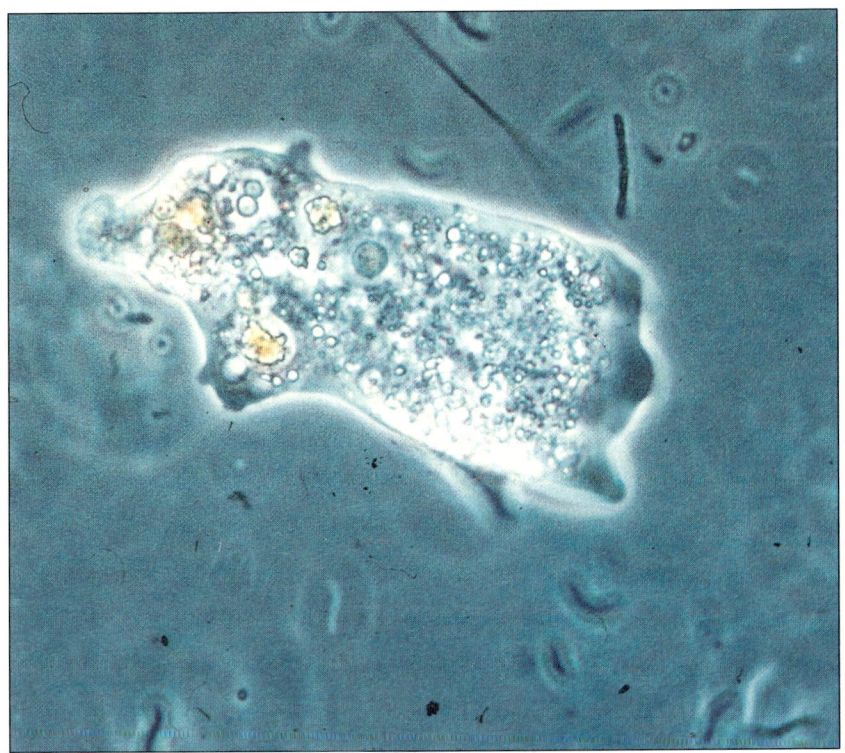

The single-celled amoeba moves part of its body around its prey, producing a "food cup" that captures food

29

Glossary

Aquatic Found in water.

Canine teeth Literally, "dog teeth," these are the pointed teeth that in humans are on either side of the four front teeth, top and bottom.

Carnivores Animals that eat only meat.

Crustaceans Creatures with hard shells and jointed legs.

Edible Suitable for eating.

Fangs Long, pointed teeth. In certain animals these are hollow, allowing poison to be squirted through them.

Habitat The surroundings in which an animal lives.

Herbivores Animals that eat only plants.

Indigestible Something that cannot be digested.

Invertebrate An animal without a backbone.

Liquefy To make into a liquid.

Mammal A warm-blooded animal with hair or fur. Most mammals give birth to babies, although a few (such as the duck-billed platypus) lay eggs. Female mammals feed their babies on milk.

Microscopic An animal or object that is so tiny that a microscope may be needed to see it.

Mollusks Creatures with soft bodies and no bones, and usually a shell to protect them.

Omnivores Animals that eat both plants and meat.

Saliva Watery fluid produced in the mouth that helps digestion.

Taste buds Special cells on the surface of the tongue that "taste" food. The human tongue has about ten thousand taste buds.

Further Reading

Bennett, Paul. *Catching a Meal.* Nature's Secrets. New York: Thomson Learning, 1994.

Parker, Steve. *The Body and How It Works.* New York: Dorling Kindersley, 1992.

Parker, Steve. *Singing a Song: How You Sing, Speak and Make Sounds.* The Body In Action. New York: Franklin Watts, 1992.

Further notes

The human mouth is quite complex. We use it for communicating, eating, and breathing. The mouths of many other animals are adapted to their needs, such as catching or eating a particular type of food. Humans can eat a wide range of foods by using tools such as a knife, fork, spoon, or drinking straw.

Parts of the human mouth

Lips—Prevent food from falling out of the mouth while eating.

Teeth—For biting and chewing food.

Tongue—To help chew and swallow food.

Taste buds—For tasting food.

Hard palate—Hard roof of the mouth.

Epiglottis—Flap of skin to close windpipe.

Windpipe—Tube that leads to lungs, for breathing.

Gullet—Tube that leads from throat to stomach.

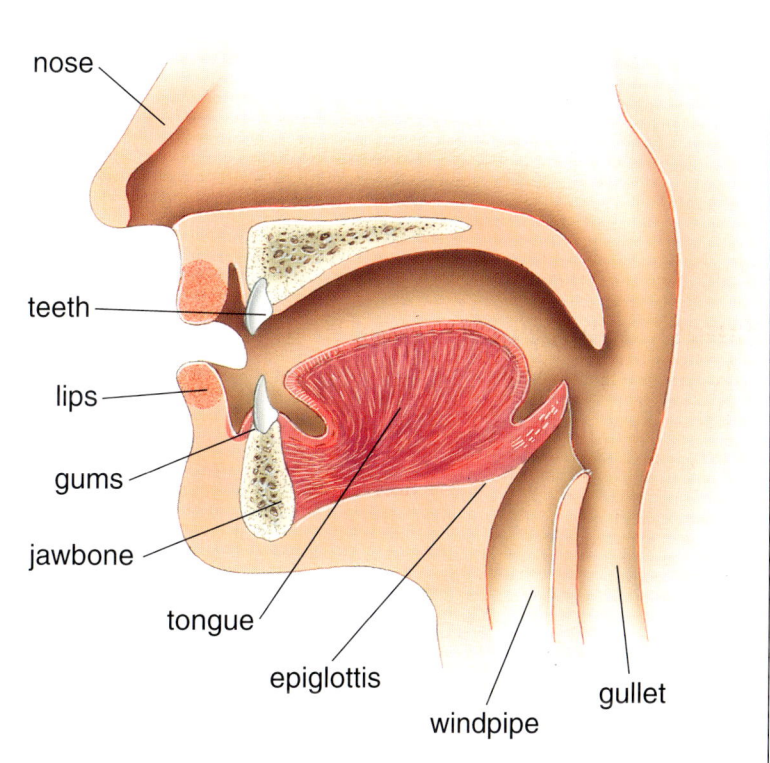

How we eat

Food is put in the mouth and chewed to make it small enough for swallowing. At the same time, glands underneath the tongue produce saliva that helps us to digest and swallow our food. The tongue is covered in taste buds to taste the food. The tongue also helps with chewing and swallowing by pressing food against the hard palate (roof of the mouth). The epiglottis (a flap of skin) closes the entrance to the windpipe so that the food goes down the gullet and not the windpipe. The epiglottis opens to allow breathing and speaking.

Our teeth

Carnivore animals have teeth for cutting and tearing meat. Herbivore animals have teeth for nibbling and grinding plants. We have a mixture of both types of teeth. The front teeth (incisors) and the pointed canine teeth are used for biting. The wide flat teeth at the back (molars) are for chewing or grinding. We use our teeth to help us chew our food in preparation for swallowing. Many animals can no longer eat when they lose their last set of teeth. Humans who lose their teeth can have false teeth made and fitted so they can continue to eat most foods.

Index

amphibians
  frogs 26
  tadpoles 26
  toads 18

birds 10–11, 25
  woodpeckers 19

carnivores 6–7, 8, 20

cruststaceans
  crabs 13
  lobsters 13

fangs 20
fish 14–16
  deep-sea swallowers 23
  devilfish 23
  mouthbreeder fish 15
  paddlefish 23
  sharks 14, 22, 23, 27

grooming (preening) 11

humans 4–5, 26, 27

insects/invertebrates
  amoebae 29
  ants 12, 13
  butterflies 16
  caterpillars 26
  dragonfly larvae 13
  fleas 16
  house flies 16
  moths 16
  octopus 11
  sea anenome 28
  spiders 21
  squid 7, 11
  wasps 13
  worms 29

jaws 12–13, 26

lips 5

mammals
  aardvarks 19
  antelope 8
  bats 20
  duck-billed platypuses 11
  lions 6, 7, 8
  monkeys 9
  rabbits 9, 27
  rhinoceroses 9
  walruses 26–27
  whales 7, 22
  zebras 8

mollusks
  clams 16
  mussels 16
  sea snails 9

reptiles
  chameleons 18
  crocodiles 24
  iguanas 9
  snakes 12, 20

saliva 19
starfish 28
sucking 16–17, 20

taste buds 4, 5, 6
teeth 4, 5, 26
  canine 6, 26–27
  incisor 8, 27
  molar 8
tongue 4, 5, 6, 18–19, 24–25, 26
tube mouths 16–17, 26